MW00943823

Luna Garza

ACCIDENTAL DETECTIVE

BONE HILLS

PJ GRAY

Luna Garza

ACCIDENTAL DETECTIVE

Bone Hills

Coal Spell

Dream Land

Found Glory

Hindsight

Main Stage

Scent of Blue

SADDLEBACK
EDUCATIONAL PUBLISHING
www.sdlback.com

Copyright © 2022 by Saddleback Educational Publishing
All rights reserved. No part of this book may be reproduced in any form or by any means, electronic or mechanical, including photocopying, recording, scanning, or by any information storage and retrieval system, without the written permission of the publisher. SADDLEBACK EDUCATIONAL PUBLISHING and any associated logos are trademarks and/or registered trademarks of Saddleback Educational Publishing.

ISBN: 978-1-68021-979-1
eBook: 978-1-64598-778-9

Printed in Malaysia

26 25 24 23 22   1 2 3 4 5

For Carol

CHAPTER 1

STRANGE POWERS

The sun was shining in downtown Apple Glen. Mrs. Carson parked the car in front of Rothman's Fine Antiques. A banner hung in the window. It read, "25th Anniversary Sale! Apple Glen's Favorite Antique Store Since 1945."

Donna jumped out of the car and hurried toward the entrance. Her mom followed. As they went in, a bell on the door rang.

"Welcome!" a woman called. She smiled at them from behind the counter.

"Hello!" Mrs. Carson replied. "We drove

over from Wood Dale. A friend recommended your store. Do you know Jo Ann Hickman?"

"Yes, of course!" the saleswoman said. "How can I help you?"

"My daughter's senior prom is coming up. We're looking for a string of pearls."

"Oh, how special," the saleswoman replied. "So you're in the class of 1970! School dances are such fun. I remember my prom like it was yesterday."

As the two women talked, Donna turned away and rolled her eyes. Her mom loved to chat with anyone. At least this gave Donna a chance to browse.

The shop was filled with an assortment of old things. Carved wooden figurines, books, and old-fashioned oil lamps lined the shelves. One table displayed a collection of jewelry and accessories. Donna noticed a beautiful hairbrush and hand mirror. She wondered who had owned them before.

Behind the mirror sat a small, dusty jewelry box. Donna opened it and smiled. Inside was a brooch in the shape of a horseshoe. The image of a horse's head was in the center.

"Mom!" she called. "Look at this!" The gold brooch seemed made for her. Riding horses was her favorite hobby. She had once owned a horse named Goldie.

Her mother was busy chatting and did not turn around.

Donna removed the brooch from the box to examine it. She noticed that the clasp was bent. It would not fasten properly. "That can be fixed," she said to herself as she pinned it to her dress. Then she grabbed the hand mirror and held it up to admire the brooch.

Suddenly, she felt light-headed. The room seemed to get brighter. She blinked a few times while staring into the mirror. Then the store began to spin. Her head and body grew heavy. Donna had to grab the table to steady herself. When she did, the brooch fell off her dress.

Everything stopped. She was no longer dizzy. The store looked just as it had before.

"Donna!" her mom called.

She hurried back to the counter.

"I'm afraid they don't have any pearls," Mrs. Carson said. She looked at her daughter. "Are you all right? You look as pale as a ghost."

Donna forced a smile. "I'm fine," she said, her voice trembling. She glanced warily back at the brooch. "Can I wait for you in the car?"

CHAPTER 2

CHARMING

Luna Garza slumped over her desk, feeling tired. Her best friend, Amber Robbins, sat next to her. Amber rested her chin in her hand. Their teammate, Cooper Sims, stood in front of their desks. He bounced back and forth like he was warming up for a race.

It was Friday afternoon. The three of them had stayed after school for an extra hour. They had done this three times a week for the past month. This was because Luna, Amber, and Cooper had been chosen to compete in a local school competition called the Brain Strain. If they wanted to win, they needed to practice.

Their coach, Mr. Kemper, smiled at them. "Tomorrow is the big day," he said. "You have all studied hard. I'm proud of you, and you should feel very proud of yourselves."

"We do," Cooper agreed. He had been chosen as team captain. "The Apple Glen Bookworms are ready. Luna is our history expert. Amber is our science whiz. And I'm our math genius."

"Genius?" Amber snickered.

Luna grinned at Mr. Kemper. "Yes, sir," she said. "We are ready. I can't wait to beat those Brainiacs." She was talking about the team from Bosstown Middle School. That was a newer school in a neighboring town. The Brain Strain would be held at the local television studio.

Mr. Kemper looked at the clock. "We are done here. Get plenty of rest tonight. Make sure to eat a good breakfast in the morning.

I'll see you at the studio tomorrow. Be there at 9:00 a.m. sharp."

Luna, Amber, and Cooper walked together to the bike racks in front of the school. They talked about the competition. There were three possible prizes for the winners. One was a $500 savings bond. Another was a trip to Ohio's famous Goof-Off Park, an amusement park. The winners could also get a weekend at Stone Hills Ranch. That was a local horse ranch.

"If we win, do we get to choose the prize?" Amber asked.

Luna shook her head. "Remember what Mr. Kemper said? There will be a big wheel on the stage. One of us will spin it. Where it stops will determine the prize."

"I hope it's not the ranch," Amber said. "You know how afraid I am of horses. That would be more like a punishment than a prize."

"My dads would never let me go there," Cooper added. "I have bad allergies to horses."

"I hope we win the trip to Goof-Off Park," Luna said. "I've never been there."

Luna and Amber unlocked their bikes. Cooper noticed Amber's keychain.

"What's that?" he asked.

Amber held it up. It was a tiny metal horseshoe. "This is my good luck charm. My uncle gave it to me for my birthday. Horses freak me out, but I'm a big fan of luck. I'm bringing it tomorrow."

"Cool!" Cooper smiled. "I have a lucky charm too. Check it out." He pulled up his pant leg. Amber and Luna looked down at his ankle.

"Socks?" Luna said. "You have lucky socks?"

Amber tried not to laugh.

"Yes!" Cooper blushed. "These socks *are*

lucky. Look at them. Can't you see the little horses?"

Luna made a face. "That's what makes them lucky?"

"Yes." Cooper looked annoyed. "Our school mascot is a horse, Luna."

"Hey!" Amber squealed. "My lucky charm is a horseshoe! I see the connection." Then she turned to Luna. "Do you have a lucky charm?"

Luna shook her head.

"Could you find one by tomorrow?" Cooper asked. "Then we'll have three times the luck for the competition."

"Find something with a horse on it," Amber added.

A horn honked. One of Cooper's dads waved from a nearby car. "I've got to go," Cooper said. "See you tomorrow!"

Amber hopped on her bike. "I have to go

too. My mom wants me home early for dinner. Bye!"

Luna watched Amber ride off toward her house. She stood alone for a few moments, thinking. *I need a lucky charm with a horse on it by tomorrow. Where can I find that?*

CHAPTER 3

LUCKY FIND

As Luna pedaled her bike, she breathed in the fresh air. The afternoon sun felt good. She decided to ride through downtown Apple Glen. This was not her usual way home. But she kept thinking about what Amber and Cooper had said. Luna did not want to let them down. Maybe she could find a lucky charm before the competition.

Just before she reached the town square, Luna stopped to text her mom.

"I'm on my way home. Just stopping downtown really quick!"

Luna looked at the shops along Main

Street, thinking. Her life had changed so much recently. The Garza family had moved to Apple Glen, Ohio, about a year ago. Her parents wanted to start a new adventure. They bought a big, old two-story house, but it needed a lot of work. While Luna's dad traveled for his job, Mrs. Garza fixed up the house. Then she used what she had learned to start her own business. Restoring old furniture and antiques for people became her passion. This was a useful skill in Apple Glen. It was a faded American town that had lots of character but could use a little polish.

Luna walked her bike in front of a few stores. "Hardware store?" she asked herself. "No, that won't work." She passed a clothing shop and shook her head. Then an old, rusted sign caught her eye. It read, "Rothman's Fine Antiques. Since 1945."

When she got to the store, Luna looked in the window. *Fine antiques?* she thought. *It looks more like a junk shop.* Then one of her mom's favorite sayings popped into her head. *Never judge a book by its cover.* Luna locked her bike to the nearest rack.

The store's front door was heavy and hard to open. Once inside, Luna noticed a young man behind the counter. He sat on a stool and stared at his phone. His hair was in a ponytail, and he wore a wrinkled T-shirt. The sign above him announced vintage clothes for sale. When Luna came in, he did not look up.

She slowly walked through the store, scanning for something that could be a good luck charm. All she saw were racks of old clothes and shelves of dusty books.

"Hey," the man said after a few minutes. Luna turned and looked at him. "There's more stuff in the basement. The stairs are behind you."

"Thanks," she said. It was clear that he didn't really care if she bought anything.

Luna went down to the basement and looked around. The whole room smelled old. Near a large, shabby sofa was a table covered in vases and jewelry. Luna picked up a few items, but nothing had a horse on it. Then she noticed a small jewelry box.

"What's in here?" she whispered while opening it.

"Wow!" A shiny gold brooch rested in the satin-lined box. It was a horseshoe with a horse's head in the center. "This is perfect!" Luna closed the box and raced upstairs.

The man at the counter looked up. Luna placed the box in front of him. It had no price tag on it.

"How much?" she asked.

He thought for moment. "Ten bucks?"

"What?" Luna scoffed. "Ten dollars? No way! Just look at it. It's not even real gold."

Luna pulled the brooch out of the box.

That's when she saw that the clasp on the back was bent.

"And the clasp is broken," she added.

"Okay." The man sighed. His phone buzzed with a new message. He did not want to argue with her. "Five bucks."

"One dollar," she said firmly.

"Fine. Deal."

Luna handed him a dollar bill. Then she put the box in her pocket and rode her bike home.

CHAPTER 4
RANCH RUMORS

Dinner is almost ready!" Mr. Garza called from the kitchen.

Luna was sitting on her bed upstairs. "Coming!" she called back.

She had just gotten home with her new lucky charm. The jewelry box with the brooch inside sat on her nightstand. Luna thought about showing it to her parents. But she remembered that her mom had once said good luck charms were silly.

"Miss Luna Garza!" her mom yelled. "Please come set the table. Ann will be here soon."

Luna raced downstairs to help. Their neighbor, Ann Watson, was coming over for dinner. Ann was a fun dinner guest. She always seemed to share something Luna didn't yet know about Apple Glen.

When Ann arrived, they sat down to eat. The conversation quickly turned to the Brain Strain competition. Luna's parents were very proud. They had been telling everyone they knew that Luna was going to be on TV.

"We're going to the studio tomorrow to watch," Mrs. Garza told Ann.

"How exciting! Luna, are the teams competing for prizes?" Ann asked.

Luna nodded. She explained the three options and how the winning team would spin a wheel to find out their prize. "Goof-Off Park sounds fun," she said. "That's the prize I'm hoping for."

"I understand offering a savings bond," Mr. Garza said. "And a trip to an amusement park makes sense. But a weekend at a horse ranch?"

"I've never heard of Stone Hills Ranch," Mrs. Garza added. "Have you, Ann?"

"Oh, it's funny you should ask! I've been volunteering at the Apple Glen Senior Center every Tuesday. Just last week, Sylvia, one of the employees, mentioned that the Stone family wants to develop the land next to the center. I asked who that was, and she told me about their ranch. It's about ten miles outside of Apple Glen. The family has owned the land for over 100 years. They breed and sell Pinto horses."

"Interesting," Mr. Garza said. "Is it a guest ranch?"

"I don't think so," Ann said. "According to Sylvia, they are a very private family. Most people in Apple Glen don't know them. But their name is everywhere. Just look around town. We have Stone Street and Stone Park."

"Hey," Luna said. "Our school mascot is a Pinto."

"That's right," Ann said. "Sylvia mentioned that too. Apple Glen Middle School used to be called the Stone Day School years ago. The family funded its construction."

Mr. Garza passed a dish of cooked carrots to Ann. "That reminds me. I read something in the local news recently about a potential new development. Someone named Bud Stone was mentioned."

"That's who runs the ranch now," Ann said. "He wants to build condos downtown. The mayor has to approve his proposal though."

"Do you think that's why he's offering the prize?" Mrs. Garza wondered. "The publicity might be good."

"Possibly," Ann said. "Sylvia told me the Stone family has a strange past. Some people say their big ranch house is haunted."

Luna dropped her fork on her plate. "Really?"

"Please, Ann," Mrs. Garza said, looking at Luna. "Don't start talking about ghosts. Our daughter may ask a million questions. This dinner might never end."

"Mom!"

Ann laughed. "Sylvia told me one story. People think the house is haunted by a ghost in a wheelchair."

"Cool," Luna said softly.

"Some say it's the ghost of a family member who died there."

Luna thought about the prize wheel again. *Maybe I don't want it to land on the amusement park after all.*

CHAPTER 5

WRITING ON THE WALL

The full moon cast shadows outside Luna's bedroom window. She changed into her nightgown and yawned. It had been a long day.

Even though she was tired, Luna's mind was busy. The Brain Strain competition was tomorrow morning. How prepared were the Bosstown Brainiacs? Could her team beat them? At least Luna had managed to find a good luck charm just in time. Amber and Cooper would be happy.

Ann's comments from dinner were also on her mind. The Stone family seemed very mysterious. Was their ranch really haunted? Why were they offering a prize in the competition? Luna found herself wishing to win the trip to the ranch even though she knew Amber and Cooper didn't want it.

After climbing into bed, Luna plugged in her phone and set it on her nightstand. The small jewelry box with the horse brooch inside sat next to it. Luna took out the brooch. "Bring us luck tomorrow," she whispered to it. Her eyelids closed as her head hit the pillow. She still had the brooch in her hand.

A moment later, she felt as though the room was spinning. Her body felt heavy. That was the last thing she remembered.

Luna slowly sat up in bed. With her eyes still closed, she carefully pinned the brooch onto her nightgown. Then she gathered her long, dark hair and put it up in a knot on top of her head. As Luna got out of bed, the sheets fell to the floor. Her eyes remained closed as she walked to her desk and picked up a wide-tip black marker.

Luna reached up and began writing on the wall. Her arm was stiff as she drew a big, thick *W*. In the same way, she wrote three more large letters on the wall. Then she climbed back into bed and fell into a deep sleep.

Knock, knock, knock.

"Are you still sleeping, Luna?" Mrs. Garza asked from outside the bedroom door. "It's time to get up. If you're not out in five minutes, I'm coming in."

Luna opened her eyes and yawned. She was surprised to see it was morning. It felt like she had just gone to bed.

Then she remembered what she had done right before she fell asleep. She sat up and opened her hand. *Where is the brooch?* she thought. *I was holding it when I fell asleep.* Luna noticed her bedsheets on the floor. *Maybe it fell down there.*

As she rolled out of bed to look, her head felt strange. She reached up and touched the top of it. *Why is my hair up in a knot?*

Once she was up, it only took Luna a moment to find the brooch. It was lying on the floor between her bed and the desk. "There you are," she said, bending to pick it up. When she stood, she noticed the bedroom wall. A word was written there in thick black letters. Her eyes grew wide.

"What is that?" Luna gasped. It was hard to read. *Does it say WAIT?* she wondered. The *I* looked more like an *L* to her. But *WALT* made no sense.

The bigger mystery was how it got there. "Did Mom or Dad do this?" Luna whispered. She shook her head. *They would never do this, even as a joke.* The next thought was chilling.

Did I do this? When? Her head felt like it was spinning again.

"Luna!" her dad shouted from downstairs. "Are you dressed yet? Breakfast is ready!"

Luna put the brooch back into its box. Then she jumped into action. The first thing she had to do was hide the writing on the wall. A poster hung over her bed. She took it down and pinned it over the strange word.

The rest of the morning was a blur. Luna took a quick shower and got ready. Then she scarfed down her breakfast. Her family had just enough time to make it to the television studio. Luckily, Luna remembered to put the brooch in her pocket before they left. All of her focus was now on the Brain Strain.

CHAPTER 6

BRAIN STRAIN

The Garzas arrived at the TV studio with no time to spare. Luna rushed up to the stage and took a seat behind her team's table.

"Phew, you made it!" Amber whispered. "We thought you had gotten into an accident or something."

"Sorry," Luna said in a hushed voice. "I woke up late." She wanted to show Amber her good luck charm, but there was no time.

Mr. and Mrs. Garza were too late to find seats. They had to stand in the back. Mr.

Kemper turned and waved to them from the front row. He did not look pleased.

Soon the show began. The TV station's weather reporter was the host. He introduced both teams and explained the rules. Each player had a bell. Whoever rang their bell first could answer the question. If they were correct, their team received a point. An incorrect answer gave the other team a chance to steal the point. Questions came from five categories: math, language arts, science, history, and culture.

Like Luna and her teammates, the Bosstown Brainiacs were very smart. After 30 minutes of questions, the teams were tied. It was the final round. That's when the director called a short break.

"Sorry, folks," he said. "We have a small audio problem. Give us just a few minutes to fix it."

Luna, Amber, and Cooper were happy for

the break. The questions had been tougher than they expected.

Amber put her hand over her microphone and leaned toward Luna. "My brain is *so* strained," she whispered.

Cooper gave her a serious look. "The score is tied. Don't give up. We can still win this."

Luna reached into her pocket and felt the brooch. If there was ever a time she needed good luck, this was it. She pulled it out and held it tightly in her hand.

"We're ready to go again," the director called. He cued the host. "Five, four, three, two, one . . . action!"

Luna began to feel strange. Her head was heavy. The studio lights seemed to have gotten brighter. She squinted to protect her eyes. Then the dizziness started.

"Okay," the host said. "This is our final question. The first team that answers correctly will be our winner!"

Luna closed her eyes and sat up straight.

The host continued. "What was set up in 1945 to keep peace throughout the world?"

Ding! Luna rang her bell.

The host pointed to her. "Apple Glen Middle School!" he called out.

For a few seconds, Luna did not say anything. It was silent in the studio. Everyone waited for her answer. Then she spoke in a soft, deep voice. "In the ground," she said.

Cooper and Amber turned to her. They looked shocked. Luna's parents exchanged confused glances. Mr. Kemper's mouth fell open.

"Could you repeat that, please?" the host asked.

Luna's eyes remained shut. She sat very still. "In the ground," she repeated in the strange voice.

"Oh, I'm sorry. That is incorrect," the host replied. He turned to the other team.

"Bosstown Middle School, you can steal this for the win."

One of the Brainiacs leaned into her microphone. "The League of Nations," she answered.

"No! I'm sorry. That is incorrect," the host said. He turned back to Luna's team. "Apple Glen Middle School, you have a second chance. Here's the question again: What was set up in 1945 to keep peace throughout the world?"

Ding! Cooper rang his bell.

"The United Nations?"

"That is correct!" the host cried. "Apple Glen Middle School is this year's Brain Strain champion!"

The audience cheered. Cooper raised his arms in victory. Then he reached for Amber's arm and raised it too. Amber smiled and grabbed Luna's hand. When she did, the brooch fell to the ground.

Luna's eyes opened. "What's going on?" she said, looking startled. Amber couldn't hear her over the crowd's applause.

The huge prize wheel was pushed onto the stage.

"Cooper Sims," the host said. "As team captain, you get to spin the wheel." The audience cheered again. Luna was still confused. She didn't remember the last question. *Did we really win?*

Cooper stepped forward and spun the wheel. Round and round it went. Finally, the wheel slowed to a stop.

"Congratulations!" the host said. "You and your team have won a weekend at Apple Glen's very own Stone Hills Ranch!"

The audience clapped. Luna smiled. Cooper and Amber did too. It was the polite thing to do.

CHAPTER 7

MEMORY LAPSE

After the show, Mr. Kemper and the parents gathered in the studio. They were all so proud of the kids. While they chatted, Cooper and Amber pulled Luna aside.

"What happened?" Cooper asked. "'In the ground?' What kind of answer is that?"

Luna was confused. *What is he talking about?*

"Leave her alone, Cooper," Amber said. "We were under a lot of pressure up there. Here, Luna." Amber pulled the brooch out of her pocket and handed it to Luna. "You dropped this. I think you were holding it when we won. Is it your good luck charm? Why didn't you tell us?"

The brooch! Luna thought. *Holding it is the last thing I remember before the end of the competition.* She took it from Amber and slipped it in her pocket.

"I didn't get a chance to really look at it," Amber added. "Was that a horse's head on it?"

"Yes," Luna replied. "I found it at an antique shop yesterday. It's nothing special."

"Can I see it?" Cooper asked.

Luna's mind was racing. She had been holding the brooch when she fell asleep the night before. Then she woke up to the strange writing on her wall. Pulling the brooch out during the competition was the last thing she remembered before her team won. But her teammates seemed to be saying she answered a quiz question that she couldn't remember.

"Come on," Cooper went on. "Show us."

"No!" Luna snapped. One thing was clear to her. The brooch must have special powers. But she did not understand them yet. She definitely couldn't risk letting her friends hold it.

Cooper looked hurt.

"Sorry," Luna said. "It's very fragile. The clasp needs to be fixed. I'll show you later."

CHAPTER 8

WELCOME TO THE RANCH

A lot went on in the weeks after the Brain Strain event. The show aired on local television. Cooper, Amber, and Luna felt like celebrities at school. But Luna was even more confused watching herself answer the final question incorrectly. She couldn't figure out what had happened. Luna felt ashamed for letting her teammates down. At the same time, she wanted to know what "in the ground" meant. Why had the brooch made her say that?

There was also the issue of the prize. Just as Cooper predicted, his dads would not let him go to the ranch for health reasons. Amber refused to go because of her fear of horses. The show's producers didn't want them to walk away empty-handed. Instead, they offered them each a $500 savings bond.

Luna, however, was excited to go to the ranch. The trip was planned for a weekend when her parents were going to a wedding. They arranged for Ann to take Luna to the Stone Hills property.

"Thanks for driving me," Luna said to Ann in the car.

"No problem." Ann was happy to help. Secretly, she also hoped to meet one of the Stone family members while she was there. Her friend at the senior center had filled her in on more rumors about the mysterious family.

"It's too bad your friends aren't coming," Ann said to Luna. "Are you okay with going alone?"

"Yes," Luna said. "I've always wanted to ride a horse. Besides, it's no big deal. The trip is just one night. My mom was worried. I told her that I'm not a baby anymore."

Ann smiled. "I know. You're growing up fast. By the way, did you pack everything you'll need?"

Luna nodded. Her bag held clothes, extra shoes, and her toothbrush. The brooch was in there too. After the Brain Strain, she had put it back in its box and left it there. It had a special power that Luna did not yet understand. But there was no way she could leave it at home. What if her parents found it? She couldn't risk anyone else holding it and blacking out like she had.

Soon Ann and Luna reached Stone Hills Ranch. The land was green and lush. Tall, old trees dotted the hillsides. It looked like the perfect place to raise horses.

"Wow," Luna said as they pulled into the

driveway. In the distance, the stately main house appeared with its red brick exterior. "It's a mansion."

"You can say that again. I would hate to clean that place!" Ann joked.

She stopped the car at a large iron gate. Ann reached out her window and pressed a button on a stone wall.

"This is Ann Watson," she said into a speaker. "I spoke with Bud Stone earlier. Miss Luna Garza is with me." Suddenly Luna felt very important.

The gate opened. Ann drove through it slowly.

When they reached the house, a man dressed like a cowboy greeted them. He shook Ann's hand first and then Luna's. "Welcome to Stone Hills Ranch," he said with a smile.

"Thank you, Mr. Stone," Ann replied.

"Oh, I'm not Bud Stone. My name is Jimmy Fipps. I'm the stable master here. Bud is my boss." Then he grinned at Luna. "And you must be the prizewinner."

"Yes, sir," she replied.

Jimmy escorted them to a small building next to the main house. It looked like a business office. "I have some papers that need signing."

"Papers?" Luna asked.

"Yes. This is a standard agreement," he said, holding up a paper and pen. "All it says is that we are not responsible if you're injured here. But don't you worry. We don't expect any accidents. You will be perfectly safe."

Luna raised her eyebrows and looked over at Ann.

Ann nodded. "It's okay, Luna. Your parents know about this. They asked me to sign on their behalf." After signing, Ann turned to Jimmy. "Will I be able to meet Mr. Stone?"

"I'm afraid Bud is on a business call," Jimmy said. "It could be another hour or so."

"What plans do you have for Luna?" Ann asked in a motherly tone.

"Don't worry," Luna said. "I'll be fine."

"Well, let's see," Jimmy started. "We want her to have the full Stone Hills experience. Today she will get a tour of the ranch. I'll show her the stables and introduce her to the horses. Then we'll get her on one. Tonight there will be a campfire dinner in her honor. Tomorrow she'll have another chance to ride the horses before she leaves."

Ann looked at Luna. "How does that sound?"

"Great!"

Jimmy led Luna and Ann into the house. He showed them the room where Luna would sleep. Ann asked to use the bathroom. While she did, Luna opened her bag and pulled out the small jewelry box. She put it in her pocket for safekeeping.

After Luna got settled in her room, Jimmy

gave her and Ann a brief tour of one of the stables. Ann wanted to meet Bud Stone, but he never appeared. Finally, she hugged Luna and left the ranch.

CHAPTER 9

FAMILY HISTORY

After Ann left, Jimmy brought Luna back to the main house. "Mr. Stone would like to meet you soon," he told her.

He opened two huge doors that led to a very large room. "Here is the Portrait Hall," he said. "This is where Mr. Stone receives guests. Have a seat. He will be here in a minute." Jimmy closed the doors behind him.

Luna was excited and a little nervous. After what Ann had told her, both the house and Mr. Stone had an air of mystery about them. While waiting, she looked around the room. It was furnished with beautiful sofas and chairs. Red velvet curtains were draped around the large windows. Her eyes roamed over the paintings on the walls. People in fancy clothes stared back at her from the gilded frames.

The huge doors opened again, and Bud Stone entered. He was a tall, older man. Luna thought he looked like a movie star from a black-and-white film.

"Hello. You must be Luna. I'm Bud Stone," he said, offering his hand for Luna to shake. "We are so glad you could come. Have you been enjoying yourself so far?"

Luna nodded, smiling. "Yes. Jimmy introduced me to some of the horses. I can't wait to ride one."

"Then you are in the right place. Horses are our passion here at Stone Hills Ranch," Bud said. "I noticed you were admiring the paintings," he went on. "These are members of the Stone family. Would you like to know who they are?"

Luna remembered the rumors Ann had shared about the family and the ghost in the wheelchair. This was her chance to find out more. "I would love to," she said.

He stepped near a painting and looked up at it. "This is Walter Stone and his wife, Mary. They were my great-grandparents. Mary came from a wealthy family in New York. She and Walter wanted to build a ranch, so they bought this land. But Walter died in World War I. After his death, Mary kept the ranch and ran it herself."

"Wow," Luna said. "That must have been hard."

"Yes," he agreed. "But she was a strong woman."

Bud walked to the next painting. "These

were Mary and Walter's three children. Edna was the oldest. Her sister, Doris, was the youngest. Their brother, in the middle, was Walter Stone Jr. He was my grandfather. Everyone called him Walt."

An image popped into Luna's mind at the mention of the name *Walt*. She felt a chill run down her back. *The word on my bedroom wall,* she thought. *Did it say Walt?*

"Out of those three, Walt was the only one to have a child." Bud pointed at a painting with three people in it. "Here is Walt and his wife, Nelly. She was my grandmother. Unfortunately, she died before I was born. The child on her lap is my father. His name was also Walter. He was the third Walter Stone in the family. My grandparents called him Trey."

Luna thought for a moment. "That sounds like the Spanish word for the number three."

Mr. Stone smiled. "Yes, that's where the name came from. Very good."

Luna blushed with pride as they stepped to the next painting. It showed a young man riding a Pinto horse.

"Is that you?" she asked.

He nodded. "Yes. I'm the fourth Walter Stone. My mother nicknamed me Bud."

Luna looked at the paintings again. "Is there a portrait of her?"

Bud cleared his throat. For a moment, he looked uncomfortable. "My parents split up when I was a child," he said without emotion. "She moved to New York, and I was sent to boarding school."

"So you didn't grow up here at the ranch?" Luna asked.

"No," Bud said. "I moved back a few years ago. It was just before my father passed away. He had a heart condition."

"Do you have any children, Mr. Stone?"

"No. I never married or had any children."
Then he changed the subject. "So, Miss Garza,
what do you know about horses?"

"Not much. I've never ridden one. But I
like to read about them."

"Oh, you like books?"

"Yes, sir."

Bud smiled. "In that case, follow me."

They walked down a long hallway to
another set of doors. "Welcome to the library,"
Bud said as he opened them.

Luna's eyes grew wide. Every wall of the
room was filled with rows of books. She stared
at them in awe. It was the home library of
her dreams.

"I would like to introduce you to someone,"
Bud said. "This is Doris Stone. She is my
great-aunt."

Across the room, an elderly woman in a

wheelchair sat quietly reading a book. She looked up and smiled at Luna and Bud.

Luna gasped. Ann's comment at dinner came rushing back to her. "The ghost in the wheelchair," she whispered to herself.

CHAPTER 10

FAMILIAR FACE

Sunlight streamed through a window and hit Doris from behind, making her glow. Her thick white hair was pulled into a tight bun on top of her head. She wore a long black dress and a string of white pearls.

"Aunt Doris," Bud said. "This is the young lady I mentioned. She won our prize from the quiz show."

"Don't just stand there," Doris said. "Come closer so we can chat."

Luna tentatively stepped forward and introduced herself.

"Goodness, child," Doris said. "You act like

you've seen a ghost." Luna blushed. It was as if Doris had read her mind. "I may be old, but I'm not dead yet. Please have a seat next to me." Doris smiled.

"You have something in common," Bud said. "Both of you love books. That should give you plenty to talk about. Now please excuse me. I need to take care of some business."

Doris and Luna talked about their favorite stories and authors.

"You have so many books here," Luna said. "Have you read them all?"

"Probably," Doris replied. "This library is my favorite room in the house. I have lived here most of my life. Do you know what a phobia is?"

"I think so. It's when you are really scared of something, right?"

"Yes. I have a phobia of leaving the house."

Luna nodded. "I see. May I ask how old you are?"

"A lady should never reveal her age. However, I will tell you that I was born in 1918. You do the math."

"Wow!" Luna said. "You are over 100 years old."

Doris smiled.

"You must have read a lot of books," Luna added.

Doris laughed, but it turned into a cough. She reached for the water glass next to her. It was empty. Then she picked up a small bell and rang it.

A door opened, and a woman carrying a pitcher of water entered. She wore a simple dress and was only as tall as Luna. The woman walked up to Doris and poured water into her glass.

"This is Miss Rita," Doris said after she had taken a sip. "She has been my helper for many years."

Miss Rita stared at Luna without speaking.

"Don't mind her," Doris said to Luna. "Miss Rita doesn't speak. She never has." Then she turned to Miss Rita. "Please bring more finger sandwiches for our guest. And fetch my jewelry box from the bedroom."

Miss Rita nodded and left the room.

Doris turned back to Luna. "I have something for you."

A moment later, Miss Rita returned with the jewelry box. She handed it to Doris and quietly left again. Doris opened the polished wooden box and pulled out a gold hair clip. Then she handed it to Luna.

Luna examined it. She could not believe her eyes. The hair clip matched her brooch.

"I want you to have it," Doris said. "It was my sister's. Her name was Edna."

Luna wasn't sure how to react at first. "Thank you very much. This is so generous. I saw your sister in a painting. She was very pretty. Mr. Stone showed me all the family portraits."

"Did he?" Doris asked. "And did he tell you what happened to her?"

Luna shook her head.

Doris became very serious. She explained that Edna had disappeared in 1928, when she was 18 years old. At the time, Doris was only 10. Their brother, Walt, was 16. Before she disappeared, Edna had confessed a secret to Doris. Edna was in love with a poor stable boy on the ranch. His name was Clem. He disappeared on the same day. The family then learned the truth of their love affair.

"We all believed they ran away together," Doris said. "Edna let me borrow that hair clip the day before she disappeared. I never saw her again."

"There's something I need to show you," Luna said softly. "I hope it won't upset you."

She pulled the small jewelry box from her pocket and opened it. The gold brooch inside clearly matched the hair clip. Both had the same image of the horse's head.

Doris put her hand over her mouth in shock. "That was Edna's brooch. Where on earth did you find it?"

CHAPTER 11

GONE BUT NOT FORGOTTEN

I bought it at an antique shop in Apple Glen," Luna answered. She was afraid Doris might reach for the brooch and want to hold it, but she didn't.

"Ah, that makes sense," Doris said. Then she told Luna what had happened after Edna disappeared.

"My mother was so upset. She became very ill. It was all too much after losing my father. Even though my brother was only 16, he became the man of the house. Walt convinced our mother to send me to boarding school in New York. After that, I moved to France to study art. My mother died while I was there. That's when Walt took over the ranch. He married a woman named Nelly. They had a son and named him after our father. His nickname was Trey."

Doris sighed before going on. "Walt must have given Edna's things away. When I returned years later, there was nothing of hers left. Somehow this brooch made it to the shop where you found it. I remember that there was a bracelet too. They all matched. Edna loved that bracelet. She wore it every day."

"Wow," Luna said. "Did Walt or Nelly explain why her things were gone?"

"No," Doris said. "Nelly couldn't. She was already dead. Did Bud mention *that* when he told you about our family?"

Luna felt the hairs on the back of her neck stand up. She shook her head.

Why was Doris confessing so much to

Luna? Perhaps she had held in so many memories for too long. Now she had to let them out.

"Nelly fell down the grand staircase in this house. Walt and the police said it was an accident. I wasn't here when she died, so I will never know for sure."

Luna thought about what Ann had said at dinner. *People think the house is haunted by someone who died here. Could it be Nelly?*

"Why did you come back to the ranch?" Luna asked.

"Walt suffered a heart attack and passed away. My nephew, Trey, needed help running the place, so I returned. That is when my phobia took hold. I haven't left this house since."

Luna then remembered what Bud had said. His father, Trey, had a heart condition. It seemed like a pattern with the men in the Stone family.

Doris was tired from so much talking. She rang her bell for Miss Rita.

"It has been lovely chatting, dear," she said to Luna. "I'm afraid I need to go rest for a bit."

Miss Rita came and wheeled Doris away. Then Jimmy entered the library from another door. He smiled at Luna.

"There you are!" he said. "Are you ready to ride some horses?"

CHAPTER 12

SADDLE UP

As Jimmy and Luna walked to the main stable, a strong breeze blew around them.

Luna spotted a man holding a large camera near the stable entrance.

"That man is from the local newspaper," Jimmy told Luna. "He's here to take your picture."

The photographer waved as they walked up. He reached out and shook their hands. "I'm Rick Cole," he said. "From the *Apple Glen Daily News*."

Rick smiled at Luna. "You are one of the

winners of the Brain Strain competition, correct?"

"Yes, sir," Luna said, smiling back at him. She began to feel bad that Amber and Cooper weren't there. What would they think when they saw her picture in the newspaper?

"Let's get you on a horse," Jimmy said.

After looking at a few horses, Jimmy picked the one that he thought would be best for Luna. It was a beautiful tan color with large white markings. He placed a saddle on the horse and showed Luna how to mount it.

Once she got on, Luna felt nervous and excited. It was her first time on a real horse.

Rick Cole was snapping photos. "Mr. Cole?" Luna said, pulling her phone from her pocket. "Would you mind taking one with my phone too, please?"

"Of course!" He took several pictures. Then he handed the phone back to her.

Jimmy held the reins of Luna's horse and walked it slowly out of the stable. Rick took a few action shots.

"Thanks," he said when they had made it outside. "I have what I need. Nice to meet you both. Enjoy your ride!" He waved as he left the stable.

"Let's tour some of the grounds," Jimmy said. "Once you're comfortable, you can take the reins. I picked a very gentle horse for you. So, tell me, Luna. Do you know anything about Pinto horses?"

"I read a few things," Luna said. "They are not solid-colored. Pintos are known for their markings."

"That's right," he replied. "Did you know there are actually four types of Pintos? They are Stock, Hunter, Pleasure, and Saddle."

Jimmy went on to give her a lesson about Pinto horses. Luna tried to listen but couldn't focus. All she could think about was the Stone family. Everything she had learned seemed to connect somehow.

She felt the brooch in her pocket and thought about its power. Then she thought about the matching hair clip from Doris. These had belonged to Doris's sister, Edna. *What happened to her?* Luna wondered.

Their brother was named Walt. Luna believed that's what she had written on the wall when under the brooch's spell. Doris had told her about the death of Walt's wife, Nelly. *Why did Doris say she never knew if Nelly's death was an accident? Does she think her brother had something to do with it?*

Suddenly, Luna remembered the answer she gave at the competition when she held the brooch. *What could "in the ground" mean?*

Jimmy's laugh pulled Luna out of her thoughts. "Don't you get it?" he asked. "*Mane* event? That's just a little horse humor."

Luna smiled and forced a laugh. "I get it. That's a good one. I'll share it with my friends at school." Then she looked around and noticed a small building near a grove of trees. It appeared old and rotted. "What's that?" she asked, pointing.

Jimmy pulled the reins tight to stop Luna's horse. "That was one of the first small stables ever built here. Now it's just an empty shed. No one uses it anymore."

Luna felt a strange chill go through her. She did not want to get any closer to the building.

"For some reason, Mr. Stone won't let us tear it down," Jimmy added. "I guess it's just part of the Stone Hills Ranch history."

The wind had picked up. A strong gust blew dust in their faces. Luna's horse was getting upset. "I think we've got a windstorm coming," Jimmy said. "We should head back."

CHAPTER 13

CHANGE IN PLANS

Jimmy led Luna's horse back to the main stable. When they got there, Luna saw a few ranch hands feeding and grooming the horses. After the spooky feeling she got on the grounds tour, it was nice to see some other people. There had been mention of a campfire dinner that night in Luna's honor. *Will the ranch hands be invited?* she wondered.

With all the wind outside, going into the main house was a welcome break. The sun was setting, and Luna felt hungry. It was time to get ready for dinner.

As she walked to her bedroom, she heard a voice. Bud Stone stood near the entrance to the library. He was talking on his cell phone. Luna stopped and listened.

"I'll get you the cash," he said. "You know money has been tight lately. Business is slow, but it will pick up soon. The city council votes in two weeks. Having that girl here will give us some good press. Today a photographer came and shot photos."

Luna remembered what her dad had said at dinner before the Brain Strain. Bud Stone wanted to build something new in downtown Apple Glen. It seemed Mr. Garza was right. The prize was a publicity stunt.

Bud did not notice Luna. She tiptoed upstairs to her room.

After getting cleaned up for dinner, she

heard a knock on the door. Miss Rita entered and handed Luna a note from Jimmy. It read: "Campfire dinner moved to tomorrow night due to windy weather. Sorry!"

"Wait," Luna said. "It can't be tomorrow night. I'm only staying here tonight. I leave tomorrow."

Miss Rita did not react.

"What am I supposed to do for dinner?" Luna asked.

Miss Rita gestured that she would bring dinner to Luna.

"Here? I'll eat dinner alone in the bedroom?"

The woman nodded.

Luna thought for a moment. "What about Doris? May I have dinner with her? I would like to see her again."

Miss Rita shook her head. She pulled a notepad and pencil out of her apron pocket.

Taking a nap, she wrote.

"Okay," Luna replied. "What about Mr. Stone?"

No. He eats alone.

Luna rolled her eyes. "Really? How about Jimmy or any of the ranch hands?"

Rita sighed and scribbled, *Gone for the day. Return tomorrow.*

"Wow. What an exciting trip."

Rita shrugged. Then she wrote that she would return with dinner.

Luna wished Amber and Cooper would have joined her. She felt lonely and reached for her phone. First she looked at the pictures of herself on the horse. Then she sent her favorite one to her mom and dad.

Mrs. Garza texted back right away. "Love this!"

Luna knew her parents were still at the wedding, but she tried calling her mom anyway.

"Hi, Luna!" Mrs. Garza answered, sounding surprised. "I thought you were only going to text back. Are you having fun?"

"Sort of," Luna replied.

She told her mom about meeting Doris Stone. "I really like her," she said. Then she mentioned the newspaper photographer, Bud Stone's phone call, and the canceled dinner. "It's all a big publicity stunt, Mom," Luna sighed.

"Do you want to come home now? I can call Ann to pick you up."

Luna thought about it. She pulled the brooch's jewelry box from her pocket. Then she got out the matching hair clip from Doris. As bored as she was, leaving did not seem right. There were still so many questions in her head. "Thanks, Mom," she said. "But I want to stay tonight. I'll find something to do."

As Luna was saying goodbye, the bedroom

door slowly opened. It was Miss Rita holding a tray of food. She placed it on the desk and pointed to a phone. Gesturing to the numbers on the phone, she held up one finger. Then she pointed to herself.

"I should dial 1 if I need you?" Luna asked. Rita nodded and left the room.

A bowl of soup and a sandwich sat on the tray. There was a bottle of water too.

"So much for a campfire dinner," Luna said to herself. She was so hungry that she no longer cared though. The soup and sandwich tasted good.

By the time she finished, night had fallen. Strong winds continued to blow. The trees outside the window swayed. Sometimes they tapped on the glass. Luna wondered if they were trying to get her attention.

CHAPTER 14

TAKING CHANCES

Luna's dinner dishes sat on the desk. She did not want to go to sleep yet. *Is it too early to snoop around the house for more clues?* she wondered. *Mr. Stone may not be asleep. And what about Miss Rita? Who knows if she ever sleeps?*

Luna looked around the bedroom. It was filled with beautiful carved wooden furniture. Near the desk, books sat on a shelf. Many seemed to be mysteries. Luna picked one. "The Hammond Boys," she whispered. That was an old mystery series. Her dad had mentioned reading these books as a child.

But Luna was not in the mood to read. She put the book back.

The small jewelry box containing the brooch was on the nightstand. Luna picked it up and sat on the bed. Part of her wanted to take the brooch out. But she was worried. She thought about what had happened when she held it before. First she wrote on a wall. Then she said something that made no sense. Everything seemed to be tied to this place. That was the strangest part.

Maybe the brooch could lead me to answers, Luna thought. *But I could lose control of my mind and body. What if I get hurt?*

It was risky. But there was something odd about this ranch. She decided it was a chance worth taking.

Luna carefully removed the brooch from the box and lay down on the bed. With her eyes closed, she waited.

Nothing happened at first. Then the

dizziness returned. It felt like the bed was spinning. She tried to open her eyes. A blinding light made it impossible. Her body felt like it weighed a thousand pounds.

That was the last thing she remembered.

CHAPTER 15

SLEEPWALKING

Luna rose slowly from the bed. Her eyes remained shut. She grabbed her shirt collar and pinned the brooch on it. The broken clasp did not close completely, but the brooch stayed on. Then she pulled her hair up with her hands and made a knot. Finally, she grabbed the hair clip off the nightstand and used it to pin her bangs back.

The house was quiet and dark except for a few dim hallway lights. Luna left her room and tiptoed downstairs. No one noticed her.

She reached the living room and walked

past the family portraits. There was a soft glow from the moonlight coming in the large windows. Outside, wind whipped through the trees. Their shadows danced on the walls.

Luna stopped at the painting of Bud Stone seated on a horse. She pulled the side of the picture frame. It opened like a door to reveal a safe in the wall.

With her eyes still shut, Luna reached for the dial on the safe. She turned it left to a number and stopped. Then she turned it right to another number. After stopping on three more numbers, she heard a click. The door opened.

Luna reached into the safe and pulled out a framed black-and-white photo. It was Walt and Nelly on their wedding day. Carefully, she removed the frame's backing. A piece of paper had been slipped in between it and the photo. The paper was old and yellowed. Luna gently peeled it off and placed the framed photo back in the safe. Then she turned and walked out of the room.

Step by step, Luna made her way up the grand staircase and down the hall. She reached a bedroom door and slowly turned the knob.

Doris's afternoon nap had thrown off her bedtime. She was reading in bed when she heard the door open.

Luna stood in the doorway.

"Who's there?" Doris asked. She leaned over and reached for the eyeglasses on her nightstand. "Good heavens, child. What are you doing here? Are you all right?"

"Have you been in the safe?" Luna said in a low voice.

"What?" Doris's heart was beating fast.

"Have you been in the safe?" Luna asked again, stepping closer.

"Safe? What do you mean? Did Bud show you the wall safe downstairs?"

Luna walked to the side of the bed. "Walt," she said. Her voice was still low.

The girl was acting very strange. It scared Doris. She tried to remain calm. "Walt? Are you talking about my brother?"

That's when Doris noticed something. Luna's eyes were closed. *Is she sleepwalking?* Doris wondered. Then she saw the brooch on Luna's shirt. The matching clip was in her hair.

"Walt pushed Nelly," Luna said.

Doris gasped. She looked closer at Luna. "No. It can't be," Doris said. Her body began to shake. "Edna, is that you?"

Luna dropped the old, yellowed paper on the bed.

CHAPTER 16

DARK SECRETS

Doris watched Luna walk out of the room.

"Wait," she said. "Where are you going?"

Luna did not respond.

Doris turned her attention to the old piece of paper. It was a short letter.

Walt,

I want my freedom and my son. Grant me a divorce and the money I demanded. If you don't, I will go to the police and the newspapers. Everyone will find out that you killed Edna and her boyfriend. And I will tell them where you buried their bodies.

Nelly

The letter trembled in Doris's hands. She began to put the pieces together in her mind.

Nelly must have written the letter to Walt before she died. If what she wrote was true, Edna did not run away. She was murdered by her brother. Walt must not have wanted his sister to marry a poor ranch worker. That would have been a scandal.

Doris remembered how Walt had convinced their mother to send her to boarding school. Had he wanted to keep her from finding out his secret? He knew Edna was not coming back, so he rid the house of her things. His wife, Nelly, must have found out about the murders somehow. Then she tried to use that knowledge to blackmail Walt. But it didn't work. Walt pushed her down the staircase to her death.

"This letter was in the safe all these years?" Doris whispered.

As a little girl, she saw her father use the

safe. When she came back to the ranch, she had once asked Trey for the combination. "There is nothing in that old safe," he had said. "Don't worry about it."

Bud had told her the same thing years later. Had they known about Walt's dark secrets?

Doris felt weak from shock. She reached for the phone next to her bed and called Miss Rita. "I need you," Doris said. "Hurry."

CHAPTER 17

WIDE OPEN

After leaving Doris's room, Luna walked back downstairs. She paused at the bottom of the staircase. This was where Nelly had fallen to her death years ago.

Outside, the wind was stronger. Its howls could be heard throughout the mansion.

Luna walked down a hallway. She passed Bud's office. He was still working at his large carved desk. When she went by his open door, he glanced up.

"Miss Garza?" Bud said. Luna did not stop.

He got up and stepped into the hallway.

"Luna?" he called again. "May I help you?"

Bud watched her turn into the kitchen. He followed her.

"Miss Garza, please wait. Where are you going?"

As he entered the kitchen, a gust of wind blew through the room. The kitchen door was wide open. Luna was gone.

CHAPTER 18

INTO THE NIGHT

Miss Rita rushed into Doris's bedroom. She took the older woman's hand and tried to calm her.

"This is all too much," Doris said. She wiped a tear from her eye. "Rita, hand me the phone please. I need to call Bud. Is he here?"

Miss Rita grabbed the phone. Something outside the window caught her eye. It was Luna. She was walking away from the house.

A worried expression came over Miss Rita's face. She looked at Doris and pointed to the window.

"What is it?" Doris asked. "Is something outside? Help me up."

Miss Rita gently pulled Doris out of bed. They watched Luna disappear into the dark night. Then they saw Bud. He was following her.

Doris picked up the phone and called the police.

CHAPTER 19

IN THE GROUND

Luna was running down a trail that passed the main stable. Bud called out to her again.

"Miss Garza! Stop! Where are you going?"

The wind drowned out his voice. Then he heard loud banging coming from a second stable along the trail. Its big, heavy door had blown open. Inside, the frightened horses neighed.

Bud rushed over to close and lock the door. When he turned back toward the trail, Luna had vanished.

Even though her eyes were still closed, Luna easily found her way. Her feet seemed to know the path. The trail turned again. She stopped. In front of her was the old stable that Jimmy said was used as a shed.

A rusted padlock was on the door. Luna grabbed it in her hands. With a burst of strength, she ripped the lock off the door.

Luna stepped into the dark shed. There were some rusty tools inside. She picked up a shovel and began to dig into the dirt floor.

When Bud reached her, he was out of breath. A sense of shock overcame him. In all his years on the ranch, he had never been inside the shed.

"What are you doing?" he screamed at Luna. "Stop!"

Luna didn't look up. She just kept digging in the same spot.

Bud realized he had to stop her. His father had told him that a secret was hidden there. It was why the shed could never be torn down. "If the truth comes out," his father had said, "our family business will be ruined." His grandfather, Walt, had told Trey the same thing. Nobody ever said what was inside, but Bud knew he had to keep it hidden at all costs.

In a moment of panic, he grabbed a large wrench that was next to the door.

Luna had finished digging and dropped her shovel. She knelt down and reached into the hole. Then the brooch fell off of her shirt collar. Her eyes opened at last.

In her hand, she saw Edna's gold bracelet. It was coated with dirt.

Bud's face turned red with rage. He could not control himself. "I told you to *stop*!" he screamed, lifting the wrench over his head.

Luna turned and noticed Bud for the first time.

"Freeze!" a voice yelled. "Police! Drop the weapon!"

Squinting, Luna saw the shape of a man

in the shed's doorway. He was pointing a gun at Bud Stone.

Stunned, Bud dropped the wrench. Then he grabbed his chest and fell to the ground.

CHAPTER 20

TRUTH COMES OUT

Mr. and Mrs. Garza got to Stone Hills Ranch a short time later. The sheriff's deputy had called them. They hugged Luna tightly as soon as they saw her. She was in the kitchen with several officers and Doris. Miss Rita had made everyone tea.

Bud Stone had been taken away in an ambulance. He had suffered a heart attack. It seemed unlikely he would make it.

The police had questions for Doris and Luna. Doris held Edna's bracelet as she talked to them. She showed the deputy the blackmail letter.

"My sister wore this bracelet the day she disappeared," Doris said. "I believe my brother, Walt, killed Edna and her boyfriend, Clem. You will find their bones in that old stable. I'm sure of it."

Doris thought that Edna's spirit had been in Luna while she was sleepwalking. But she knew nobody else would believe that. It would have to stay a secret between her and Luna.

"I found the letter in the safe," she told the officers. "Luna stumbled upon the shed while she was exploring the grounds. The poor dear knew nothing about this whole mess."

One of the officers handed Luna the brooch. "This was found on the ground," he said. "Do you recognize it?"

At first, Luna was afraid to hold it. But Doris's eyes told her it would be okay. Luna clutched it tightly in her hand while the others talked. She felt nothing. The brooch's power was gone.

Luna had come out of her strange sleep. The clues made sense at last. Walt was behind Edna's disappearance. For many years, her story had been buried in the ground. But now the truth was out. Edna was finally at peace.

EPILOGUE

Bud Stone died that night. The local paper ran an article about Stone Hills Ranch after his death. It included a photo of Luna on horseback during her visit. Some of the Stone family history and scandals were mentioned. But Luna knew so much more.

Doris Stone was finally able to overcome her phobia. She left the ranch and moved to an assisted living facility. The Garza family visited her there once. Her health was declining. But she was in good spirits. Luna wore Edna's brooch and hair clip. That made Doris smile. It was the last time Luna saw her alive.

After Doris's death, a few months passed. Then the Garza family received a letter from a lawyer's office. It explained that Doris had donated the ranch to a local charity. Children with disabilities would be able to ride horses and receive therapy there.

Mr. Garza was proud to show Luna the end of the letter. It stated that Doris had named the house's library the Luna Garza Reading Room.

Enclosed with the letter was Edna's bracelet. Doris had wanted Luna to have the whole set.

Luna Garza

ACCIDENTAL DETECTIVE

THE MYSTERY CONTINUES . . .

Bone Hills
9781680219791

Coal Spell
9781680219920

Dream Land
9781680219944

Found Glory
9781680219784

Hindsight
9781680219760

Main Stage
9781680219777

Scent of Blue
9781680219807